CLIFTON PARK-HALFMOON PUBLIC LIBRARY

W9-AHO-103

For Sophie, Roman & Lauren

First published in 2012 by Child's Play (International) Ltd
Ashworth Road, Bridgemead, Swindon SN5 7YD UK

Published in USA by Child's Play Inc
250 Minot Avenue, Auburn, Maine 04210

Distributed in Australia by Child's Play Australia Pty Ltd
Unit 10/20 Narabang Way, Belrose, NSW 2085

Text and illustrations copyright © 2012 Jo Empson
The moral right of the author/illustrator has been asserted

All rights reserved

ISBN 978-1-84643-552-2
L050912CPL11125522
4065
Printed and bound in Heshan, China

1 3 5 7 9 10 8 6 4 2

A catalogue record of this book is available from the British Library

www.childs-play.com

Clifton Park - Halfmoon Public Library
475 Moe Road
Clifton Park, New York 12065

Nothing exciting ever happens to me!

Never, ever!
Humph...

...Never, ever, does anything exciting EVER happen!

Never, ever...

...ever, never... ...any excitement!

Never, ever...

Ever?

Never!

Never, ever, ever, ever, ever, ever, ever, ever...

ROAR!

ever, ever, ever...

...never, ever, ever, evereverevereverevereverever

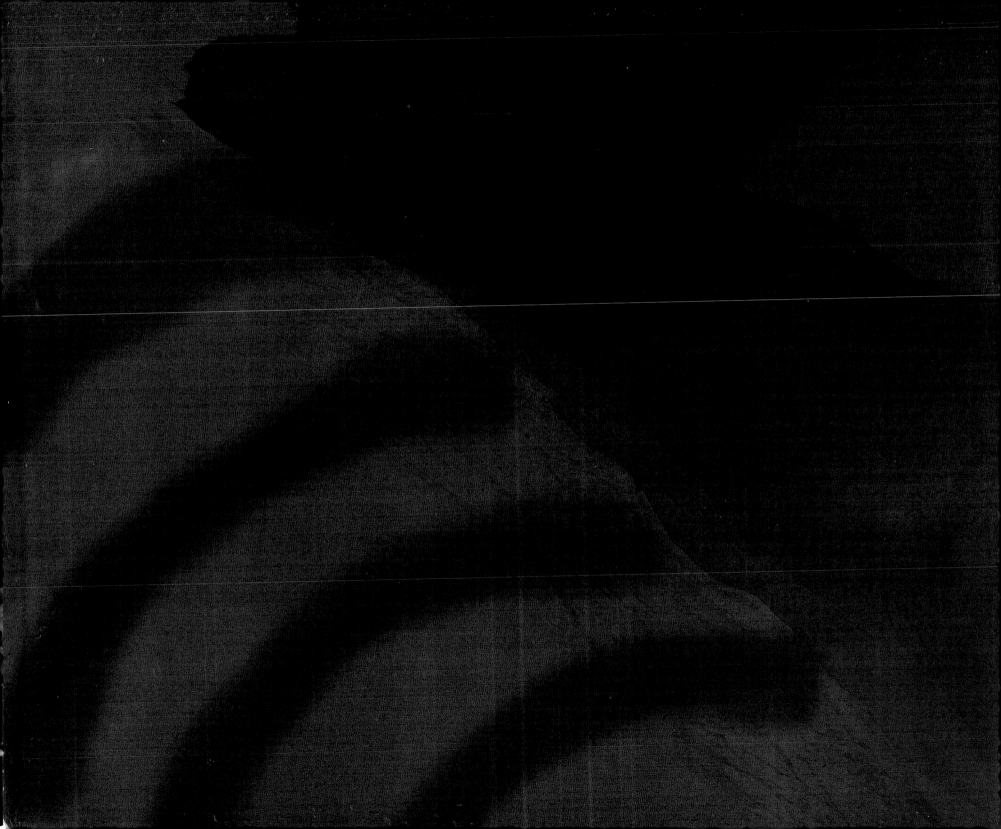

See? Told you!
Nothing exciting
EVER happens to me!

...ever, ever...

Never ever...